Madison to the Country

Written by Melanie Martin
Illustrated by G. Brian Karas

Troll Associates

Library of Congress Cataloging-in-Publication Data

Martin, Melanie.
   Madison moves to the country / written by Melanie Martin;
illustrated by G. Brian Karas.
     p.   cm.—(Fiddlesticks)
   Summary: Madison A. Mouse makes a surprising discovery after
moving from the noisy city to the peaceful country.
   ISBN 0-8167-1345-6 (lib. bdg.)   ISBN 0-8167-1346-4 (pbk.)
   [1. City and town life—Fiction.   2. Country life—Fiction.
3. Mice—Fiction.] I. Karas, G. Brian, ill. II. Title.
III. Series.
PZ7.M36412Mad 1989
[E]—dc19   88-1313

Madison A. Mouse lived beneath the biggest skyscraper at the busiest corner of a great big city.

The A in Madison's name stood for "Avenue." Isn't Madison Avenue a perfect name for a big-city mouse?

Madison's home was nearly perfect, too. His roomy apartment was tastefully decorated, and each room was filled with soft furniture. The cozy living room even had a working fireplace.

But Madison was unhappy living where he did. He had grown tired of big-city life.

"I'm sick of the city," Madison groaned, as he peered through his window. "I've lived here all my life. There must be some place better than this."

What was wrong with Madison's home? For one thing, the noise.

"The big city is too noisy," Madison complained.

Indeed it was!

In front of Madison's building, workers were tearing up the street. A jackhammer was pounding away at the pavement. RAT-A-TAT-TAT! RAT-A-TAT-TAT! RAT-A-TAT-TAT! All day long went the jackhammer. RAT-A-TAT-TAT!

"Here we go again," Madison grumbled, as the pictures on the wall began to shake. Then the furniture began to jump around the room. Madison, too, began to shimmy and shake as the jackhammer thundered away.

"I can't stand this anymore," Madison cried. "A mouse needs some peace and quiet!"

Madison put on his hat and went out the
front door.

"Maybe a walk will calm my nerves,"
he said, as he started down the sidewalk.
He hadn't gone far when a car came by and
hit a puddle. SPLASH! A spray of water shot
into the air. Madison was soaked!

"Thanks a lot," Madison yelled, shaking
his fist angrily at the passing car.

Mumbling and grumbling, Madison
walked on. He turned at the corner and
stopped at the curb to check the light.
It changed from green to yellow. Madison
had to wait before crossing.

Traffic started to move. CRASH! A delivery truck bumped into the back of a yellow taxicab. The accident blocked the intersection. Instantly, traffic backed up. Car and truck horns began to beep. HONK! HONK! HONK! Drivers were yelling impolite things. It was a terrible traffic jam.

Madison covered his ears.

"Honking! Yelling! Crashing!" cried Madison, as he walked away. "City life is anything but peaceful."

As he turned another corner, Madison spotted a familiar face. Melanie Mouse was walking toward him. Madison and Melanie were old friends.

Madison stopped to chat about the accident. "Hello, Melanie," said Madison, "you'll never guess what just happened."

Melanie smiled but didn't stop. "I don't have time to guess. I don't have time to talk," she explained, as she hurried past. "There's a sale on cheese at Bloomingdale's department store. I've got to get there before they close."

She rushed by so fast Madison didn't have the chance to say another word.

"That's another thing I hate about city life," Madison grunted. "Everyone is always too busy. Rush here! Rush there! City mice always get caught up in a rat race!"

Madison started walking again. He felt
sad. His tail dragged wearily as he started
home. When he neared his block, Madison
glanced at his watch.

"Five o'clock," he said. "Good! Those
workers will be going home now. I won't
have to hear any more jackhammering until
tomorrow."

Madison stopped in his tracks. He gulped.
"Five o'clock?" he sputtered nervously.
Madison had just remembered what he hated
most of all about city life. "RUSH HOUR!"
he screamed, as he raced off in a panic.

Suddenly, the doors to office buildings
began to open. Waves of people flowed out
into the street. Soon the sidewalk was
crammed with crowds of workers rushing
home.

"Gangway! People stampede! Look out!" Madison yelled. He scooted around feet and in between legs.

A high-heeled shoe nipped past his nose. As he ducked a pair of sneakers, his hat fell off. It was squashed flat by an orange work boot.

Darting from here to there, the little mouse inched his way toward the safety of his front door.

"Made it," he sighed, as he slipped the key in the lock. He opened the door and popped in, as a flood of feet rushed past. "This is the last straw," said Madison.

That night Madison made an important
decision.

"I'm moving to the country, and I'm never
coming back," Madison vowed. "Country life
is quiet, calm, and easy. In the country
everyone is friendly, and there are no rush
hours. Tomorrow Madison A. Mouse moves
to the country."

Early the next morning, Madison left his apartment with a suitcase in his hand. He tacked a For Rent sign on his door and walked off toward the open-air market.

Every morning, farm trucks came to the city to deliver fresh vegetables and fruit to the market. After the trucks were unloaded, they drove back to the country. Madison planned to hitch a ride on one of these trucks.

At the market Madison hid behind a wooden box and peeked out. He saw a shiny green pickup truck. It was just getting ready to leave.

"There's my ride," whispered Madison.

He sneaked out of his hiding place. Ever so quietly he crept toward the truck. As the driver started the motor, Madison climbed up a stack of boxes. He tossed his suitcase into the back of the truck and jumped in after it. The little mouse landed on a bale of straw.

"Hooray!" he cried as the truck began to move. "I'm off to the country."

As the morning sun climbed into the sky, the truck drove down one street after another. On and on it went until the big-city skyscrapers got smaller and smaller and farther and farther away. Madison sprawled on the straw and enjoyed one last look at his former home.

"Good-bye, city," the little mouse said. "I won't miss you one bit."

With a smile on his face, he closed his eyes and fell into a peaceful sleep.

Hours later, the truck turned off the highway onto an old dirt road. It went BUMPITY-BUMP as the tires bounced in and out of potholes.

"Hey!" yelled Madison. He was suddenly awake. "What's going on?"

BUMPITY-BUMP! BUMPITY-BUMP! Madison bounced around the back of the pickup like a furry, gray ball.

Suddenly, the truck screeched to a stop. Madison tumbled toward the front of the pickup. BONK! He bumped his head.

"Ouch!" groaned Madison, rubbing a lump on his furry noggin. "That was as bad as a subway ride."

Madison shook the cobwebs out of his head and then looked around. There were trees, hills, and rolling pastures all about.

"I'm in the country!" he exclaimed joyfully.

Madison climbed up to see why the truck had stopped. A gaggle of geese was blocking the road.

"Move, geese," ordered the driver of the truck. "Move it!" Impatiently, he tapped on the truck's horn. BEEP! BEEP! BEEP!

The geese refused to budge. They began to honk in reply. HONK! HONK! HONK!

BEEP! HONK! BEEP! HONK!

"Oh no," sighed Madison as he covered his ears. "I didn't think they had traffic jams in the country, too!"

At long last, the stubborn geese made a path for the truck. Off it sped toward a farm just ahead. It came to a halt in the middle of a huge barnyard. There was a white house, a big red barn, and a tall, shiny silo.

"This is my new home," Madison said, as he collected his suitcase. He climbed out of the truck and skipped over to the barn.

Madison looked all around. Behind an old rain barrel he discovered a crack in the side of the barn. He peeked in and found a small hole. It was just the right size for a mouse.

Madison moved right in. His new home wasn't very cozy. It was dusty and gloomy. "It will look better when I get some new furniture," Madison told himself.

After he unpacked his suitcase, Madison
set out to hunt for furniture. It wasn't an
easy task. Poor Madison had to make do
with anything he could find.

A big flat rock became a table. Two white
pebbles were used for stools. He bound up
some twigs with string to make an easy chair.
An old thimble became a vase for wild
flowers. Madison looked at his apartment.
Despite all his work, it still looked dingy.

"I guess I'll get used to it," Madison sighed. "Now I need some straw for a bed." He ran out of his house and scooted into the barn. Inside he found something that surprised him.

"A cow!" he exclaimed. "A real, live country dairy store. Since we are going to be neighbors, I might as well introduce myself."

Madison strutted over to the cow's stall.

"Hi, neighbor," he shouted, waving up at the cow in a friendly fashion. "I'm Madison A. Mouse."

The cow didn't answer. She was too busy munching on grain to pay any attention to a pesky little mouse.

Madison didn't like being ignored. He climbed on the milking stool beside the cow. In an angry tone he shouted, "Hey, you stuck-up cow! I'm Madison, your new neighbor!"

The cow continued to eat. Without even turning her head, she whipped her tail in Madison's direction. SWAT! The tail hit Madison. "Yipes!" he cried, as he toppled off the stool into a pail of milk.

SPLASH!

"Glub! Glub!" Madison blubbered, as he sloshed around in the bucket. "I hate milk baths!"

The little mouse grabbed the edge of the pail and pulled himself out. He dropped to the barn floor and shook himself dry. "Rude cow," he grumbled as he stormed off to gather straw for his bed.

By the time Madison finished making his
bed, the day was done. As the last rays of sun
faded, the barnyard became pitch-black.
There were no city lights to brighten the
night.

"I'm starving, but it's too dark to look for
food," Madison said as he rubbed his empty
tummy. "I wish there was an all-night deli
around here." He went sadly to bed. Soon he
was sound asleep.

The next morning Madison was abruptly awakened by an old familiar sound. RAT-A-TAT-TAT! RAT-A-TAT-TAT!

"What is that?" grunted Madison. "Jackhammering in the country? It can't be!"

RAT-A-TAT-TAT! RAT-A-TAT-TAT!

Madison raced out his front door and looked around.

RAT-A-TAT-TAT!

Clinging to the side of the barn was a bird with a red head. It was using its beak like a jackhammer to peck holes in the wood.

"Who are you?" demanded Madison. "And what are you doing?"

The bird stopped pecking. "I'm a woodpecker," the bird answered. "I'm hunting for insects. Now, excuse me, but I've got to get back to breakfast."

RAT-A-TAT-TAT! RAT-A-TAT-TAT!

Madison couldn't believe his ears. Morning in the country wasn't as quiet as he thought it would be.

"Breakfast," said Madison as his stomach rumbled. "That sounds like a good idea. I'm starved!"

33

Madison began to hunt for food. Near
the back of the barn he found a tall hickory
tree. Nuts were scattered on the ground
underneath it.

"I like nuts," Madison said as he picked
one up.

Just then a gray squirrel scrambled out of
the tree and rushed toward Madison.

"Hi!" said Madison as the squirrel
approached. "My name is Madison. Would
you like to join me for breakfast?"

The squirrel rushed right by the little mouse. "No time to chat," called the squirrel, scooping up an armful of nuts. "Winter is coming. I've got to gather food. Can't stop now." The squirrel darted back past Madison and ran up the tree trunk. With a flick of his fluffy tail, he vanished into a clump of leaves.

"You can have breakfast with us, little mouse," someone called.

Madison turned around. He saw a smiling, pink pig poking its snout through the rails of a pen.

"Thank you, Mr. Pig," said Madison, as he strolled over to the pen. "I'd be delighted to join you. My name is Madison A. Mouse."

"My name is Petey," replied the pig. "Come join us."

Petey pointed at a bunch of other pigs dozing near the side of the pen. "Those are my friends. We all live here together."

"Your friends look tired," said Madison.
"I won't disturb them, will I?"

Petey shook his head. "Oh no! They'll
wake up fast enough when the farmer comes
to feed us. Just wait and see."

It wasn't five minutes before the farmer came, carrying a bucket of scraps. He walked up to the edge of the pen and poured the scraps into the pig trough.

"SOOOOWEEEE PIGS!" bellowed the farmer.

Instantly, the pigs awoke. They eyed the trough hungrily and licked their lips. Without warning they made a mad dash for the food. And right in their path was Madison A. Mouse!

"Yipes!" yelled Madison, as he saw the pigs charge. "Feeding time is rush hour for pigs!"

Poor Madison! The pigs ran right over him, and he ended up face first in the mud.

"I'm sorry about that," said Petey, helping Madison to his feet. "Would you still like to join us for breakfast?"

Madison eyed the pigs as they greedily gobbled up their food. "No thanks," said Madison. "I just lost my appetite."

Madison walked back to the barn. He washed up in the barrel, then went inside his mouse hole. It looked gloomier than ever.

Madison thought about his apartment in the city with its soft furniture and cozy fireplace. He thought about all the things that had happened to him since he'd moved to the country. Then Madison began to pack his suitcase.

Before long he was ready to leave. As he
stepped into the barnyard, Madison bumped
into the squirrel he'd seen near the hickory
tree.

"Hi, neighbor," said the squirrel. "I was
just coming over for a visit. Sorry I was too
busy to talk before." Then he noticed the
suitcase in Madison's hand. "Are you going
someplace?" he asked.

Madison nodded. "I made a big mistake," he explained. "I didn't know how good I had it in the city until I didn't have it anymore."

Madison sighed. "I guess that no matter where you live, there are always good things and bad things about it. What's important is knowing where you belong. And I belong in the city."

The squirrel smiled understandingly.
"The farmer is driving a load of fresh eggs to
the city today," the squirrel said. "If you
hurry, you can catch a ride."

Madison rushed over to the truck. "Good-
bye," he called, as he climbed into the back
of the truck.

The squirrel waved as the truck drove
away.

Madison couldn't wait to get home.
As soon as the truck stopped at the open-air
market, he hopped down and rushed off. He
was never so glad to see and hear all the
sights and sounds of busy city life!

HONK HONK

CLICK

CLACK

BEEP

RAT·A·TAT

When Madison reached his apartment, he
pulled down the For Rent sign on the door.

"Madison, where have you been?" he
heard someone say.

Madison turned and saw Melanie Mouse.

"I came to visit you yesterday," Melanie
said. "When I saw the sign, I was worried.
I hope you're not moving. You're the best
friend I have in the city."

Madison opened his front door. "I'm not moving," Madison assured her. "I've been to the country, and I don't care for it at all. The city is my home."

Melanie smiled. "You must tell me about the country over tea," she suggested. "I brought you some fresh cheese."

"What a wonderful idea!" Madison replied.

The two mice walked into Madison's apartment. And as he shut the door, Madison said to himself, "It's good to be home."